A No-Fuss Christmas

A No-Fuss
CHRISTMAS

SUSAN KIRBY

journeyforth®

Greenville, South Carolina

Library of Congress Cataloging-in Publication Data

Kirby, Susan E.

A no-fuss Christmas / Susan Kirby.

p. cm.

Summary: In 1932 Oklahoma, Sueker eagerly awaits a
Christmas reunion with her brother, but feels edged out when her
foster parents make room for a homeless child until her role as
inkeeper in the Christmas pageant sheds light on the day's true
meaning.

ISBN 978-1-60682-059-9 (perfect bound pbk. : alk. paper)

[1. Family life—Oklahoma—Fiction. 2. Foster home care—
Fiction. 3. Christmas—Fiction. 4. Homeless persons—Fiction.
5. Orphans—Fiction. 6. Oklahoma—History—20th century—
Fiction.] I. Title.

PZ7.K63353No 2010

[Fic]—dc22

2009052344

Illustrations by Gabhor Utomo

Design and page layout by Peter Crane

© 2010 by BJU Press

Greenville, SC 29614

JourneyForth Books is a division of BJU Press

ISBN 978-1-60682-059-9

15   14   13   12   11   10   9   8   7   6   5   4   3   2   1

For Megan, Bryce, Meadow, and Isaiah
Thank you for the joy of grandparenting
To God be the glory

CONTENTS

CHAPTER 1

CLINTON, OKLAHOMA 1932

The front door opened. Sueker Tucker popped to her feet. But it was only Maggie, followed by a customer and a cold draft of air.

Sueker sat down on her pop crate. She emptied the dust from her shoes.

Maggie circled behind the counter and stopped short. "What're you doing?"

"Making an ant hill," said Sueker, pushing the shoe dust into a little pile.

Maggie rang up the sale.

The customer paid and went on his way.

"I wish Christmas would hurry up and get here. I wish we had a big smell-good tree and candy and presents, don't you?" said Sueker to her foster sister.

"Sure I do. But you heard Mama. Don't be expecting a big fuss," said Maggie.

Sueker's real mother had died before Sueker was old enough to remember her. Maggie's parents had since taken her into their family. It was nice to have a dad *and* a mama like other kids. But Mama's willingness to let Christmas pass without a fuss was worrisome. Did Dad feel the same way?

Sueker had come right after school to talk to him. She made believe she was an ant while she waited. Pa ant came home, lugging candy crumbs. The ant family trimmed a pine needle in popcorn and paper chains. Broken peanut shells became presents. Then along came a dust storm. *Poof!*

Sueker blew and scattered her ant hill.

"There's enough dirt without you blowing it every where," complained Maggie.

"I'm pretending there's a black blizzard," said Sueker.

"How about watching for customers instead, and I'll go home and clean up?" said Maggie.

Maggie hated dust. She wanted to be a secretary with soft hands and clean fingernails and pretty dresses. But that kind of job was hard to find these days. So she helped her father at the garage instead. It was drab work for a girl who couldn't pass the front window without looking at herself in the glass.

"Go on. I'll watch for customers," said Sueker.

"You will?" Maggie's face lit up. "Thanks, Sueker."

Whoosh! The wind pushed Maggie the moment she stepped out. Another gust caught the door. It shut with a bang.

"Is that you, Maggie?" Dad called from the back shop.

"She left, Dad. I'm staying in her place," said Sueker.

"Call me if anyone wants gasoline."

Dad was skilled with engines. He used his ears like an extra pair of hands. It wouldn't do for her to share her hopes for Christmas until he was free to listen.

Route 66 ran past the garage on its way through town. Sueker leaned one elbow on the counter the way she'd seen Maggie do. Helping at the garage made her feel grown-up. She liked watching the traffic trickle by their doorstep, but no one pulled off the road for fuel.

Dad kept working until sunset. With his permission Sueker counted the cash drawer. She didn't bother with vouchers. Folks couldn't always keep their promises anyway.

Dad tucked the day's receipts into his pocket. "Go on out while I lock up," he said to Sueker.

Sueker walked to the edge of the hard road. Dust stung her eyes. There had been no rain. The wind had sifted the soil until it wouldn't hold together.

The same was true of Sueker's real family. Her pa had died a few years back. All she had left of her beginnings in Illinois was her doll Clarisse and her brother Razz.

Razz was seventeen now, and Sueker hadn't seen him since moving to Oklahoma. Three years was a long time. If he looked her up, would she even know him?

CHAPTER 2

The wind was hoarse from shouting. It skipped dry leaves over the road. A train lumbered in the distance, whistling and chuffing steam.

"I wish Razz would come for Christmas," Sueker said as they started home.

"I can see how you'd miss him," said Dad.

"Can I write and ask him to come?"

"Better talk to Mama about it first."

Sueker dodged a tumbleweed. "What if she says no?"

"You won't know until you ask," said Dad.

Businesses lined both sides of the road. A dry goods store was open for trade. The windows were trimmed for the season with green boughs, red bows, and tinsel.

"*Some* folks are planning on Christmas coming as usual." Sueker pointed to the window.

"Can't think of anyone who isn't," said Dad.

"But Mama says there'll be no fuss."

"Not in the way that *you* mean, Sueker. She's saying one thing; you're hearing another. Take your Christmas pageant, for example. She's really looking forward to that. We all are," said Dad.

"No room!" Sueker belted out her line.

"That's our girl. The hostess with the mostest."

"Dad! I'm the inn keeper."

"Don't I know it! And I'm real proud of you for making the best of it," added Dad.

He knew that Sueker had hoped to be Mary. Or an angel shining bright.

She nearly lost her balance, searching the night canopy. "I'd like to see angels in the sky, wouldn't you?"

"Yes, . . . and Jesus coming back on the clouds of heaven," said Dad.

"He's coming back?"

"Jesus talked about it to His friends. They wrote it down so we'd know to be ready and watching," Dad told her.

It was news to Sueker. Her real pa had never talked about God the way Dad did. Unable to picture what to expect, she asked, "Will He start over and be a baby again . . . in a world with no room?"

"No, this time—"

"I got room. I love Christmas," interrupted Sueker.

"Yes, and Mama does too." Dad assured her with a smile.

Maybe she *was* hearing Mama wrong. If Mama truly loved Christmas, she wouldn't stop it from coming to their house. Or stand in the way of Razz coming.

Dad turned down a quiet dirt street. Their house was at the end of the block. But he stopped in front of their neighbor's home and opened the gate.

"I'll wait here while you check-see on Miss Tims," said Dad.

A lantern burned in Miss Tims's dark house. Sueker glanced back toward the gate before knocking.

"Good evening, Susan. You're running late this evening," said Miss Tims as she answered the door.

"Yes, ma'am. Dark comes in a hurry, and we was working."

"You *were*. Say it correctly, Susan," said Miss Tims.

"Yes, ma'am, we *were*. Can—" Sueker caught herself in time. "*May* I empty your ashes or carry some coal for you?"

"You may do both," replied Miss Tims.

Sueker turned and called to Dad, "I'm going to help Miss Tims."

"All right then. We'll see you in a bit." Dad tipped his hat to Miss Tims and went on home.

"Don't dawdle now. It would be thoughtless of us to keep your mother waiting supper," said Miss Tims.

Sueker spilled ashes on the carpet, trying to hurry.

"Get the broom and sweep them up, please," said Miss Tims.

Sueker did so, and then went to the basement for coal. It was dark and cold. It smelled like rotten potatoes.

"Hurry up, Susan. You're letting all my heat escape," called Miss Tims from the head of the stairs.

Sueker was as quick as she could be without leaving a trail of coal dust.

"I'll be expecting you after school tomorrow. You won't forget now, will you, Susan?" said Miss Tims.

She didn't suppose she was allowed to forget. Same as she couldn't insist that Miss Tims call her *Sueker*.

Respect her years, darlin'. She's from the old school where a proper name means something. Mama's words rang in Sueker's ear.

A name did mean something when there was love behind it. Sueker's birth mother had named her *Susan*. But Pa had tagged her *Sueker*. Sometimes *Sue*. But mostly *Sueker*. That's who she was and always wanted to be.

Miss Tims had a different idea. She showed her in a book that *Susan* came from the Hebrew name *Susannah*, meaning 'lily.' A lily, she said, was lovely and pure. She said it was a person's duty to live up to the name given to them by their parents.

But her real parents were gone. So what did it matter anyway?

CHAPTER 3

Frets fell away as Sueker stepped in the front door and smelled supper cooking.

"I'm in the kitchen." Mama's voice pierced the gloom of the unlit rooms between them.

Sueker made a beeline for her short, sturdy foster mother and collected a hug.

Mama cupped her cold face in her warm hands. "How was school today?"

"Fine. Where's Maggie?"

"Upstairs in her room. Did you see your letter?" asked Mama.

"I got a letter?"

"From Razz," said Mama, smiling. "There on the table. Wash up. Then you can read it while the cornbread browns."

Upon their father's death, Razz had been left in the care of the pastor back home in Shirley, Illinois. Pastor was a stickler about education. These days, Razz wrote a neat hand:

Dear Sueker,

Hunting's fair. I got my traps oiled, waiting for snow. Get a day's work in now and again. But a steady job's hard to come by. I been courting Kitty Maxwell. Her mama doesn't like me much. Says I'm just like Pa. Says it right to my face. I hold my head up and grin like it pleases me. You remember that, Sueker. Don't let folks beat you down.

Say, do you remember old Jeremiah Bishop and his young wife, Polly? Maggie's mama used to keep house for them. She looked after their little boy, Parker. You know who I mean? Maybe not. Park was just a tadpole when you moved. Anyway, he and his older brother Jere Jr. lost their folks to influenza. I figured Mrs. Tilton would want to know.

I reckon it's time I come see how much growing you've done since you became an Okie. I've got no money for train fare. But I'm coming somehow. Hope to make it by Christmas, so you be smoothing the way with your foster folks, you hear? See you soon.

Your brother,

Razz

Sueker let out a yell. "He's coming, Mama! Razz is coming!"

Mama swung around. "Coming here?"

"For a visit! Dad said I should ask. Can he, Mama? Can I write and tell him it's okay to come?"

"Yes, I suppose. If he's able to get here, he's welcome," said Mama.

Sueker squealed for joy and flung her arms around Mama. Nothing could stop Christmas now.

CHAPTER 4

Sueker shared her good news over supper.

"He's coming *here*?" yelped Maggie.

"That's right! I can't wait! How long does it take to get here from Illinois, Dad?" asked Sueker.

"That depends on how he's coming," said Dad.

"Thumbing rides would be my guess," Maggie spoke up.

"I don't care, just so he makes it here for Christmas," said Sueker.

Maggie changed the subject. "Wesley offered us a ride to pageant practice tomorrow night."

"Goodie. You can sit in the middle," said Sueker.

"I don't care where I sit. Wesley's just a friend," said Maggie quickly.

Sueker knew better. But if she teased, Maggie might change her mind about letting her tag along. Wasn't everyday Wesley got to drive his daddy's pickup truck. Anyway, she had more news from Razz's letter to share.

"Mama, you know those folks you used to work for back home? Well, Razz said that him and her both died."

Mama bolted straight up in her chair. "The Bishops? They *died*? Sueker, are you sure you got that right?"

Sueker glanced at Dad for help. He looked as stunned as Mama. Voice shrinking, she said, "It's here in Razz's letter. Wanna see?"

Mama's eyes filled with tears as she read the letter. "It's true. Mr. Bishop and Miss Polly died of influenza, Dave. I can hardly take it in."

"I'm sorry, darlin'. I know how fond you were of Miss Polly." Dad tried to comfort Mama.

"I got a letter from her last summer. All about little Parker," said Mama brokenly. Tears filled her eyes. "I helped her with him from the day he was born. Think of it! Six years old and no parents to raise him."

"It's bound to be hard on Junior too," said Dad, reaching out to Mama.

Mama dabbed her eyes with an apron corner. "Junior's never married. What's he know about raising his little brother?"

"We've been away awhile. He's surely settled down some," said Dad.

"Jeremiah Junior and Parker are half brothers, right?" said Maggie. "I kind of remember when Mr. Bishop's first wife died."

"That was a heartache too," said Mama. She excused herself then and left the table.

It was a quiet meal without her.

Later during family devotions, Mama gave into tears again. Her sorrow stirred memories in Sueker. But she refused to let old hurts steal her joy over Razz's coming visit.

Chapter 5

Sueker looked down the iron grate in the floor. She could see Mama in the kitchen below. She was taking the pins out of her hair. Most nights she hummed to herself as she brushed out her hair. But not tonight.

Sueker slipped down the back stairs.

"Are you all right, Mama?" she asked.

"Yes, darlin'. What're you doing up?"

Sueker rubbed her toe over the worn floor. "I was thinking about Christmas. Can we get a tree to decorate? Since Razz is coming, I mean."

Mama got to her feet. "Sit," she said, and motioned with her brush.

Sueker sat in Mama's chair by the stove.

Mama had a calming touch with a hairbrush. Sueker grew sleepy counting. At one hundred strokes,

Mama put the brush down. She rested her hands on Sueker's shoulders.

"I'm sure Razz means to come, Sueker. Maybe he can catch a ride this way. But if not, I just don't know how he'll come on empty pockets," said Mama gently.

"Oh, he'll come all right. He promised. Razz always keeps his word, Mama," said Sueker.

"All right then. Just so you understand what he's facing." Mama kissed her and sent her back to bed.

Before crawling in, Sueker whispered to her doll, Clarisse, "Let's say our thank-yous."

Sueker dropped to her knees and thanked God that Razz was coming. She thanked Him for her family. And she asked Him to help Mama get over being sad over the friends she had lost to influenza. "In Jesus' name, amen."

Shivering, Sueker plowed under the covers. She hugged Clarisse, thinking of presents under a bright tree, a big turkey dinner, and Razz beside her at the table.

Chapter 6

"How are you today, Miss Tims?" asked Sueker politely.

"I'm tired from cleaning up after the wind." Miss Tims plunked down in a chair and reeled off instructions.

"Yes, ma'am," said Sueker, and did as she was told.

She fetched coal. She peeled two potatoes. She beat the rugs and spread them straight.

"What's that spilling from your pockets?"

Sueker flinched at Miss Tims's crabby tone. "Paper scraps, ma'am. I found them in the trash bin behind the school."

"That explains the dust on my clean floor." Miss Tims heaved to her feet and reached for the broom.

Sueker poked her paper scraps into her pocket and fled. It had been two weeks. Surely today was the day.

But Razz wasn't there to meet her.

"Thanks for beating the rugs. Thanks for fetching coal. Thanks for peeling wrinkly potatoes," Sueker huffed and puffed.

"Is Miss Tims having a bad day?" asked Mama.

"Yes, and she's mean." Sueker repeated her critical words.

"Miss Tims is so all alone. She needs your company as much as your helping hands," explained Mama.

"I wouldn't mind if she'd just be nice," said Sueker.

"Is that what's hurt you?" Mama pulled Sueker in close and wrapped her arms around her.

"Thank you, Lord, for all the times our sweet girl has let Your light shine for Miss Tims. In Jesus' name, amen," Mama said to God.

She kissed Sueker on top of the head and let her go. It was then Sueker noticed that Mama had been cleaning house too. The floors. The curtains. The stove. Why, the whole downstairs gleamed bright as a new penny.

"Are we having company?" asked Sueker.

Mama smiled. "If that's a pat on the back, thank you, darlin'. Would you be so kind as to sweep the porch while I finish supper? Bless your heart," Mama added as Sueker took the broom.

From the porch, Sueker saw a car stop in front of the house. A dapper young man climbed out.

"Is this the Tilton residence?" he called from the street.

"Yes, sir," replied Sueker.

"Are your folks home?"

Mama came out before Sueker could answer.

"Junior! Aren't you a sight for sore eyes! Welcome to Oklahoma. Dave should be home anytime. You remember our girl, Sueker, don't you?" Mama added and drew Sueker forward.

"My. You've grown, little miss." The young man stepped up on the porch and reached for her hand.

Sueker tried to place him, but couldn't.

"How are you getting along?" Mama was asking.

"As best I can, Sophie. I sure appreciate your hos-pitality. It's been a bumpy ride. We're ready for a break."

"It's a long way from Shirley to California," said Mama.

Shirley? Shirley, Illinois? But of course. The man was Jeremiah Bishop, Junior! Clearly, Mama was expecting him. So why hadn't she and Dad mentioned it to Sueker? *Maybe he can catch a ride.* Mama's words flashed to mind. Was that it? Had Razz caught a ride with this man? Had they planned to surprise her?

Oh, happy day! Sueker bolted off the porch and hit the ground running. With each stride her knowing grew. Razz had come! He was hiding probably. Just like the old days.

Holding back laughter, Sueker opened the car door and gave a shout. "Come out, come out wherever you are!"

A No-Fuss Christmas

A little boy cowered into the far corner of the back seat.

"Where's Razz?" she called and crawled in to find him herself.

The boy fumbled the box in his lap. Jewelry spilled over the lumpy blanket on the floor at the boy's feet.

The blanket. Sueker lunged to pull the curtain on Razz's hiding place. But it was caught, and she was caught too.

Mama had her by the coattail. "Sueker Tucker! Where's your manners? Come out of there. You're scaring little Parker."

CHAPTER 7

It was a fine supper. Freshly baked bread and split pea soup with carrots and onions and summer sausage floating in it. Sueker wished it were Razz sitting there enjoying it instead of Mr. Jeremiah Bishop, Junior and his little brother, Parker.

Did Mr. Bishop have a word from Razz to pass along? Given the chance, she would ask. Meanwhile she was keeping her eye on Parker. He had a loose tooth. All through dinner, he wiggled it with his tongue. It needed pulling.

Sueker hoped for seconds. When none were offered, she took her empty plate to the kitchen. She tied one end of a string to the door leading out to the wash porch.

"If you're finished eating, you may be excused to play," Mr. Bishop told his little brother.

Parker joined Sueker in the kitchen.

"Is that tooth botherin' you?" Sueker asked him.

Parker didn't answer.

"I can pull it just like that," she said, and snapped her fingers.

Parker wiggled the tooth with his tongue.

"Are you a crybaby, Parker?" asked Sueker.

He shook his head from side to side.

"All right then, you can open your mouth," she said.

Parker was slow to do so.

Sueker hummed a lullaby the way Razz used to do. Just when she thought he wouldn't, Parker cooperated. With quick fingers Sueker slipped the slipknot over his loose tooth.

"Back up whenever you're ready," she told him.

The string was stretched as far as it would go. Sueker opened the door and swung it inward. The string went slack.

"Take a step back and hold on to the table like this." Sueker demonstrated.

Parker gripped the kitchen table with both hands.

"That's a-time," encouraged Sueker. "Ready? Here goes."

Ca-whop! She slammed the door.

Parker hollered. His tooth was hanging crooked now.

"I can fix that," said Sueker.

But Mama rushed in before she got the chance.

"Sueker Tucker! What have you done?" she cried.

"I was only trying to help," Sueker made her voice small.

"Some help," said Mama. She sat in a chair and lifted the boy onto her lap. "Steady, Parker. It's hanging by a thread. Tell me when you're ready, and I'll put it in your hand."

Mama's soothing way with Parker was unsettling. Sueker told herself she hadn't meant to hurt him. She tried to convince Parker of it. But he wouldn't answer or even look at her.

"You're in my light, Sueker. Finish clearing the table, please," said Mama.

Mama kept her word. When Sueker returned with dishes, Parker's tooth was in his hand. Mama wiped his face and took him to join the men in the parlor. Sueker wanted to warm herself by the potbellied stove too. But she had to help Maggie in the kitchen.

"I'll wash. You dry. And don't be a slowpoke. Wesley will be here soon," reminded Maggie.

Pageant practice. Sueker brightened. Mrs. O'Neida had asked the church board for money to buy a live tree. Wesley and his friends, Martin and Billy, were supposed to pick it out and set it up for the kids to decorate.

If Mama didn't change her mind, it would be the only tree Sueker would be decorating this Christmas. She wasn't about to miss out on it.

CHAPTER 8

On the way to practice Wesley had bad news. There would be no tree after all. The church board had turned down Mrs. O'Neida's request.

"But why?" cried Sueker.

"No money," Wesley replied.

Sueker could have cried.

But it hadn't dampened Mrs. O'Neida's spirits. She sent Wesley and his pals off on a secret mission. Then she called practice to order with a cheery cowboy, "H-o-w-w-wdy!"

The children responded with smiles and giggles.

"We're going to run through the pageant, start to finish," said Mrs. O'Neida. "If you forget your lines, my assistant Maggie will prompt you. Now let's get started." She sat down at the piano.

It was rough going with lots of mistakes and forgotten lines. Maggie got flustered, but not Mrs. O'Neida. She was patient and never once got cross. Afterwards she sat them on the front rows and faced them from the piano stool.

"We can make this pageant our gift to God. And we can ask Him to use it to help our parents and friends."

"How?" asked Sueker.

"Thank you for asking, Sueker," replied Mrs. O'Neida. "Christmas celebrates our great hope in Jesus. Isn't that right, children?"

Seeing her friends nod, Sueker nodded too.

"God brought Him into the world to a life of ease? No! He was born—*where* was He born?"

"A stable!" the children chorused before Sueker could get the word out.

"Yes, and it was dusty and cold and dangerous. There was a powerful king wanting to kill baby Jesus. Mary and Joseph were having a hard time. But they trusted God, and did He help them?"

"Yes," said the children.

"He certainly did." Mrs. O'Neida pulled a tired toddler on her lap.

"Sometimes life can be difficult for us too," she continued. "No rain. Farms and gardens producing poorly. Dust everywhere. Folks start feeling afraid and thinking about leaving Oklahoma, looking for a new start.

"But you see, the same God who kept baby Jesus in hard times promises to care for us too. Did you know our Heavenly Father wants to be a father to everyone of us? He loves us! When we receive His love . . . why, there's nothing to fear. Father God won't leave us. He never dies. He's as close as the air we breathe. He knows just what we need when we need it."

Sueker wondered if Mrs. O'Neida was talking about her. Was she reading her mind? How could she know the fears she'd felt ever since Pa died?

"Oh, how He cares for us," Mrs. O'Neida was saying. "Can we trust Him, children?"

"Yes!" they cried.

"Yes, of course we can. Isn't that good news? That's why we're having this pageant, to honor God. There's nothing too hard for Him."

Wesley, Billy, and Martin came in just as Mrs. O'Neida finished asking God to use their pageant to calm fears and bring people into the family of God. The boys were carrying tumbleweeds.

"Thank you, gentlemen," said Mrs. O'Neida. "We're going to use our imaginations, children. It's time to decorate for our pageant."

Sueker gathered around the tumbleweeds with her friends. Mrs. O'Neida showed them how to stick the weeds together and make a tree. They sprinkled the tree with water and then salt so it would sparkle. Then they hung colored bows and buttons and paper chains.

It wasn't as good as a live tree with fragrant green branches, but it was a brave effort. Mrs. O'Neida thanked God for the better tree they'd have next year.

Taking courage, Sueker joined hands with her friends. She circled the tree, singing "Jingle Bells," and went home, hoping Razz had come.

CHAPTER 9

Mama and Dad were entertaining Mr. Bishop in the parlor. The potbellied stove was glowing. Sueker saw at glance that Razz hadn't made it yet. She wanted to plunk down at Dad's feet, but Mama said it was her bedtime.

She got ready and crawled into Maggie's bed. Mama came up to tuck her in. She read the Golden Rule to her from the Bible, then heard her prayers and kissed her good night.

Sleeping in Maggie's room was a treat. But Sueker had left Clarisse in her own room. She'd have to get her.

Sueker crept over the cold landing to her dark room. The floor creaked as she inched to the bed and patted the covers seeking Clarisse. Was that the wind? Or was it breathing she heard? Breathing!

Sueker darted to the landing, then pivoted. Could it be Razz? Had he come while she was at practice? Was he hiding, waiting to surprise her?

"Razz? Is that you?" she whispered.

Sueker retraced her steps. Her fingers found the lamp stand . . . and then the matches. Breath caught, ears taut, she struck a spark.

Light flickered, dashing her hopes.

It wasn't Razz. It was Parker Bishop fast asleep in her bed.

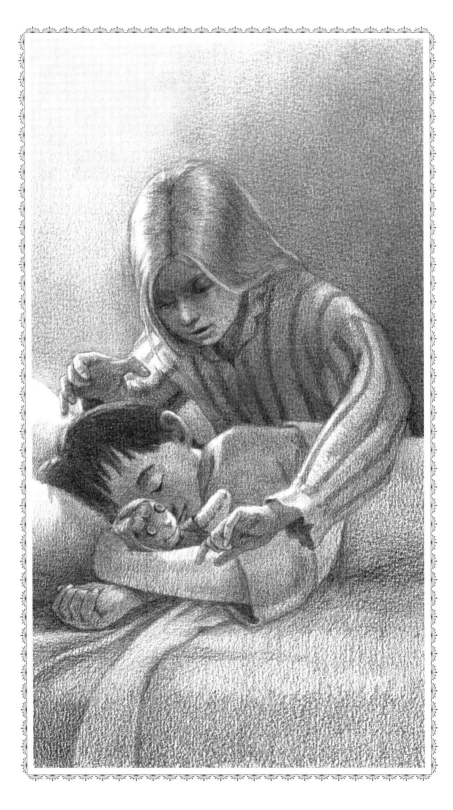

Chapter 10

Sueker struck two more matches before she found Clarisse. She was peeking from the covers in the curl of Parker's arm.

"That's my doll," Sueker said.

Parker didn't answer. Sueker reached for her doll, but he had a firm grip. She resisted the impulse to jerk Clarisse out of his arm. Mama wouldn't like it if she woke him. Sueker crept back to Maggie's room empty-handed. Warm air came up through the floor grate. It felt good on her cold feet. She could hear the grown-ups talking below, telling Maggie goodnight.

Before coming to bed, Maggie would wash her face and teeth in the kitchen where it was warm. Then she'd look at her face in the mirror for a spell.

In the meantime Mr. Junior Bishop was telling her folks how he had lost his father's farm—the equipment, the livestock, the house, and outbuildings too.

"Friends have invited me to stay with them," Sueker heard him say. "But their house is small, and they have no children. I don't know how long it'll take me to find a job."

"Is there someone to watch Parker, once you do?" asked Mama.

"No, not yet. That is to say . . ." He cleared his throat and tried again. Sueker grew uneasy listening.

Abruptly the conversation dropped to a whisper. Hearing footsteps, Sueker dived in bed. Good thing too. It was Mama, not Maggie, who nearly caught her eavesdropping on grown-ups.

"How long is that boy sleepin' in my bed, Mama?" Sueker asked straight away.

"I don't know for sure. But I want you to be as considerate of him as you'd want folks to be with you, should circumstances be reversed," said Mama.

The Golden Rule again. Sharing her room could be just the beginning. Sueker caught the top quilt between thumb and forefingers.

"Mr. Bishop could have made room for Razz in his automobile. He came all this way," said Sueker.

Mama stroked Sueker's hair back from her face. "I'm sorry you got your hopes dashed, darlin'. I know how eager you are to see Razz again."

"He'll come. I've been asking God every night to send him," Sueker confided.

"God knows what's best for all concerned," said Mama. She covered Sueker's hands with her own. "Let's pray together about Razz coming. We'll ask God to help Parker too, whatever his brother decides."

Suppose Parker stayed. What next? Would he take her pop crate at the garage? Her place at the table? How was she to hold on to what was her own?

Sueker remembered when her real father brought home a little hound-pup named Prince. Her cat Sassy spit and hissed and scratched that pup's nose. She let him know right off who was boss. In a few weeks Prince was bigger than the Sassy Cat. But he had learned his place. He ran after the barn cats and barked them up the tree. But when it came to Sassy, Prince wouldn't give chase.

Maybe there *was* room for Parker Bishop. So long as he understood that Sueker Tucker was here first. For starters, she'd teach the little hound-pup prince about leaving his hands off what belonged to her.

Sueker crossed the landing and collected Clarisse from Parker, and he never even stirred.

CHAPTER 11

The next morning Sueker dressed and went to her own room. Parker was still in his nightshirt. He turned from peeking under her bed.

"What're you looking for?" asked Sueker.

"My clothes," he said.

"Did you look in here?" Sueker bumped Parker's suitcase with her foot.

He didn't jump up and look. So Sueker opened the lid and walked her fingers through it. Curiosity satisfied, she gave him fresh clothes and went downstairs.

Dad and Maggie were eating breakfast with Mr. Bishop.

"There's biscuits and bacon in the warmer, Sueker," said Mama from the stove. She was heating water in the copper boiler. As the soap melted, it filled the kitchen with the steamy smell of washday.

Dad carried the water out onto the laundry porch for Mama. Then he left for the garage. Maggie went with him.

"You can wash the clothesline for me as soon as you've finished breakfast, Sueker," called Mama from the laundry porch.

Sueker pulled on her coat and joined her there. "Parker licked his knife and put it in the jelly."

"Leave him be, darlin'." Mama closed the door leading into the kitchen. "He can work on table manners another day."

Where would Parker be working on them? Was he going to California or wasn't he? Mama didn't say.

Chapter 12

Sueker scattered feed for the chickens. Was Razz on his way? Today could be the day. The hens bobbed their heads for seeds and cackled in agreement.

She filled their water jars.

She collected the eggs.

Then she hurried around front to check the street. There was no sign of Razz. But Parker was in the road running after his brother's car. He had his coat half on, half off. His arms got tangled up. He lost his balance and fell face first on the street.

Mama came to where Parker lay crying and gathered him in her arms.

Meanwhile Junior Bishop kept driving.

Sueker turned her eyes away from Parker's crying and Mama's loving. She crossed the yard to check-see on Miss Tims.

"You've got company," said Miss Tims.

"It's Parker Bishop here from Illinois. Mama used to work for his folks. He's staying with us for a spell," said Sueker.

"And the young man?"

"That's his big brother, Junior. Did you want the ashes emptied?" Sueker asked.

Miss Tims said, "If you would, Susan."

She wanted the particulars on Parker . . . and his parents . . . and his run-off-to-California brother. Her list of chores ran out about the same time Sueker ran short of answers.

Mama was cranking the wringer, running clothes through the rinse tub.

"How's Miss Tims?" she said to Sueker.

"Curious as can be," replied Sueker.

"Ask Parker if he'd like to help string up the wash," said Mama.

Sueker found him in the kitchen. He had a red mark on his face.

"You wanna help hang wash?" asked Sueker.

Parker didn't answer.

"You can hand me pegs," she said.

Parker put his head down on the table and stopped his ears.

"What's he doing?" asked Mama when Sueker returned to the backyard alone.

"Sitting with his fingers in his ears."

"Be patient, Sueker. Everything is unfamiliar to
him. It'll take some take. Remember how it felt when
you first came to live with us?"

Left behind and afraid. Sueker didn't say it out
loud. She knew what Mama was getting at, but she'd
have to be careful. She didn't want to lose her place.

Mama patted her shoulder and went inside to
check on Parker herself.

After lunch Sueker got out her colored-paper
scraps. She stirred flour and warm water together for
paste.

"Maybe Parker would like to help you," Mama
prompted her to ask.

"Pretend I'm the teacher," Sueker told Parker. "Put
your books away, boys and girls. It's time for art."

Sueker went on to demonstrate how to piece the
scraps together on butcher paper. "When it dries, we
will cut paper ornaments from it. Then all we'll need
is a Christmas tree to hang them on." She made certain Mama heard that part.

Parker made no move to help, so Sueker did the
paper piecing herself.

"I'm pretending it's a paper quilt. For Clarisse,"
she added.

"Very nice," said Mama. Including Parker in her
smile, she suggested they go outside and see if the
wash was getting dry.

Sueker was agreeable. But not Parker. He was a
bump on a log in a fog. Leaving her glued-up paper
to dry, Sueker grabbed her coat and went outside
without him.

CHAPTER 13

The railroad tracks skirted Sueker's back yard. Often train cars spilled coal. Sueker checked the clothesline, then called to Mama, "I'm going on a treasure hunt." She took the coal bucket with her.

The railroad embankment was steep. Sueker was dodging sticker weeds when she heard Mama call. Looking back, she saw Parker scuffing across the yard with his head down.

"Hurry up if you're coming," she called.

The embankment was steep. Parker kept sliding back. Sueker rolled her eyes the way Maggie used to do when she tagged along. "Give me your hand," she said, and helped him up the bank.

"What kind of treasure?" Parker asked.

"Coal. It spills off passing trains, and it's free for the taking."

Parker commenced to pick up three rocks for every piece of coal. Sueker showed him the difference. He did better after that.

The rail was easier on the bottom of cold feet than the rocks, but Sueker felt vibrations and warned, "Get off the tracks, Parker. There's a train coming."

The train chuffed out of the west. It belched cinders and smoke and shook the ground. Sueker spotted two men in the door of an open boxcar. It wasn't uncommon to see displaced folk traveling the country that way.

A string of coal cars followed. A young fellow was on top of one. He saw their bucket and kicked coal to them as the train carried him eastward.

Parker trampled on Sueker's feet, backing up. The young man was climbing down from the coal car! He flung his pack to the ground, jumped clear of the train, and came toward them.

"Dad's garage is just ahead. Come on," said Sueker.

But something about the way the fellow loped along made her look back. He was waving his hat. Now she could see his face. Razz? Yes, Razz! Her heart soared. He'd come at last! But what was he doing on an eastbound train?

CHAPTER 14

Sueker flung her arms around her grown-up brother. She squeezed him tight and jumped for joy. "I knew you'd come! I've been watching every day."

"Hoover flags can't stop me!" Razz said of his empty pockets.

Sueker laughed for joy. His voice was deeper than she remembered. A few brave whiskers peppered his cheeks and chin. But he was the same old Razz.

"Did you pass Clinton by?" Sueker asked.

Razz confessed it with a sheepish grin. "I woke up in Texas this morning and had to catch a train back. But it wasn't a bad trip. I rode with Junior Bishop until yesterday, when he spun off without me."

"What'd he do that for?" asked Sueker.

Razz dismissed it with a shrug. He stooped to collect his feed-sack travel pack. Together, they ran to catch up with Parker.

"Howdy, squirt. I see you've met my sister," Razz greeted him.

"You steal," said Parker, looking hard at Razz.

"There's tons of coal. They won't miss it no more than I kicked off," replied Razz.

"You took my money," said Parker.

"Your dollars are missing?" Razz stopped short. "All six of them?"

"Six dollars?" said Sueker in disbelief.

"He had 'em in a sock when we left Shirley," said Razz, nodding. He scratched his head. "Come to think of it, I don't remember seeing your money sock when Junior stopped yesterday."

"You took it and ran away," Parker said again.

"I didn't run away. I got out to stretch my legs, and Junior drove off without me," Razz told him.

"Maybe your money is in your brother's car," said Sueker to Parker.

"Or Junior could have put it in your suitcase for safekeeping," said Razz.

Sueker hadn't seen any sign of a sock with money in it when she got clothes for Parker that morning. She said as much.

"Why don't you look again?" suggested Razz.

"Good idea. I'll do that," said Sueker.

But it didn't keep Parker from sulking. Sueker had no time for him anyway. She and Razz had catching up to do. And Christmas! It was a week from tomorrow.

"It's going to be a good Christmas now that you're here. Won't be a tree though. Mama says there won't be a fuss," added Sueker.

"Money's tight. Folks do what they have to do," said Razz. He stopped and read the sign on Dad's garage. "Is this Dave's place?"

"Nice, isn't it?" Sueker beamed. "I help out, watching for customers. I can add in my head and make change too."

"When'd you get so smart?" teased Razz.

CHAPTER 15

"Well, well. Look who's here!" Dad said, shaking Razz's hand.

"Did I take you by surprise, sir?" said Razz with a grin.

Dad chuckled and confessed it. "We should have listened to Sueker. She assured us you'd come, and by Christmas too. My, it's good to see you, Razz," he greeted him warmly.

Give Maggie her dues, she was polite too. She introduced Razz to Wesley and his pals, Martin and Billy. The three boys were loafing at the garage, tinkering with an old motor.

Razz was quick to friendship. By the time they started home, he had plans to meet Martin and Billy after supper. Stores stayed open late on Saturday night. The boys promised to show Razz around town.

Mama was delighted to see Razz. She served him a bowl of soup right away and another big helping at supper. There was bread too. And fried apples.

All through supper, they talked about Shirley. The school. Old friends. The store. The church. The pastor's family, which included Razz.

Some of the news they'd already learned from Parker's brother, Junior. But Razz had a way of bringing home to life with a story. Even Maggie couldn't keep from laughing. Mama said listening to him was like a trip home.

"Yes, it is," confessed Maggie. "But I have made good friends here too."

"Isn't it the truth? God's so good to us," said Mama.

Sueker knew just how she felt. She grinned at Razz.

Looking on, Dad mused, "You know, Razz, if we'd all wait and watch for the Lord's return the way Sueker watched for you, folks would be ready for sure."

"You know I'm a man of my word, don't you, Sis?" Razz tugged Sueker's curls and grinned.

The kitchen stayed warm and damp with bath water heating on the stove. Dad built a fire in the front parlor as well. Mama determined the order of baths. Maggie went first, then Sueker. Eager to cut out Christmas decorations, Sueker was quick to return to the parlor.

Wesley Kelsey came and went, taking Maggie for a stroll downtown. Razz tagged along, planning to meet up with Martin and Billy.

Mama sent Parker to take his bath. Afterwards he looked on as Sueker made decorations out of her glued-up paper.

Mama quilted and Dad read from the Bible. Parker grew sleepy watching Sueker hang paper bells and trees and stars about the parlor. Mama helped him up the stairs to bed.

"Sueker, wrap it up. It's time for bed," she called back.

Upstairs, Sueker was drawn to the lamplight in her room. Mama sat on the edge of the bed, trying to get Parker to say his thank-yous to God.

"What're you thankful for?" Mama asked him.

To hear the silence, you'd think all Parker had to count was scrapes and bruises.

Thankful to have so many thank-yous, Sueker said her prayers and crawled in bed. Right away she missed Clarisse. She waited until Mama went downstairs to take her doll from Parker.

CHAPTER 16

The next morning Sueker raced to keep up with Razz. He held the church door for her. She was stamping the dust off her feet when she saw a sight that took her breath away. . . . Tall and wide and smelling like Christmas, a beautiful evergreen tree all but filled the foyer.

"Boy howdy. Now that's a tree!" exclaimed Razz.

Sueker could only gaze in wonder. How green and glorious!

"Maggie, look!" she cried.

Maggie gasped out loud and moved in for a closer look.

Mama and Dad arrived with Parker trailing behind them. They took a turn at being stunned. The pastor didn't know where it had come from. No one did.

"What a lovely gesture. God bless you, whoever you are," added Mrs. O'Neida. "And just in time for our dress rehearsal tonight."

After services folks took time to welcome Razz and Parker. Razz shook hands and greeted them politely. But Parker hung his head and wouldn't say boo.

Sueker circled the stately evergreen tree while her folks visited with friends.

"The tumbleweed tree makes a poor second cousin to that big bruiser, doesn't it?" said Razz to Billy and Martin.

"You want to toss it out back?" asked Billy.

"We had better ask Mrs. O'Neida first," said Martin.

Razz wrinkled his nose. "It smells like weeds."

"Leave it to a woodsman to notice," said Maggie.

"What happened to 'old dumb woodsy'?" teased Razz.

Maggie's face turned pink.

"That's what Maggie called me when she lived in Shirley," Razz said. "I was the fella she loved to hate. Wasn't I, Maggie?"

"There you go, giving yourself too much credit," replied Maggie.

Billy and Martin snickered.

Razz laughed too. "At least she hasn't lost her spunk."

Wesley came wearing a frown. He beckoned to Billy and Martin. Razz trailed after them.

"I wonder what that's about?" said Maggie.

Sueker was more interested in the tree than the boys ducking out the door. Mama and Dad had told her over and again that nothing was too hard for God. Looking at that big green answer to prayer, she knew it was true.

CHAPTER 17

It started snowing after lunch and continued throughout the afternoon. Sueker was hoping to play outdoors before pageant practice. But she had to check-see on Miss Tims first.

Parker invited himself along. But he wasn't any help. He stood on the rug and waited while Sueker emptied ashes from the parlor stove.

"Goodbye, Parker," said Miss Tims as Parker pulled on his mittens.

"Just a moment, Susan," she added before Sueker could follow him out.

Miss Tims closed the door after Parker. "I understand that a Christmas tree was found at the church this morning."

"Yes, ma'am. You should see it! The top reaches clear to the ceiling." Sueker got excited just thinking about it.

"I'm interested in learning who gave it," said Miss Tims.

"Me, too. But Dad says do good deeds in secret and don't expect a pat on the back," Sueker told her.

"There are exceptions," replied Miss Tims. Peering over her glasses, she said, "I heard voices last night, Susan. I looked out to see your brother cut across my back yard."

"But Razz was with Billy and Martin last night," said Sueker.

"Yes, I saw them make a light. Your brother went into Mr. Tilton's shed. He came out with a saw and an ax. About that time Wesley Kelsey brought your sister Margaret home. The boys left with Wesley, taking the tools."

"They probably asked Dad if they could borrow them. He doesn't care, so long as they put 'em back," Sueker said quickly.

"That's none of my concern. However, I am concerned about the windbreak out at the cemetery. My father donated those evergreen trees a few years before his death. I'd hate to think they fell to tomfoolery."

"Razz wouldn't cut a tree without permission," Sueker said quickly.

"Then you won't mind going to the sheriff's office in the morning and asking him to drive me out to the cemetery, will you?"

Sueker did mind. She minded so much, she stuck her chin in the air and refused. "I can't. I'd be late for school."

"Very well then. Run along, Susan," Miss Tims dismissed her.

Pinpricks danced before Sueker's eyes as she let herself out. She remembered what Razz said about kicking coal off the train yesterday: *There's tons of coal. They won't miss it.*

What if he reasoned one tree among many would never be missed?

"What're you going to do?" Parker hurried to keep up as Sueker scuffed through the snow.

"About what?" said Sueker.

"The tree."

"You have ears like a hound pup,"

"She talks loud," said Parker.

"Yes, and she's mean," said Sueker with heat.

It silenced Parker. But Sueker hadn't forgotten his accusation concerning Razz and his money sock. *First money disappeared, and now a tree showed up mysteriously.*

Sueker flung herself down in the snow. She cleared the ground, making fast, furious snow angels.

Parker dropped beside her. His angels were a poor imitation.

"I can do it better. Faster too. You're just a pup," she told him.

"I'm not a pup. I'm Parker."

"Then quit copying me." Sueker's anger spilled over.

Parker got to his feet and went inside.

It didn't help. Nothing would except to prove that Razz was innocent. But how? Sueker grew cold thinking about tree fellings and what to look for.

CHAPTER 18

Sueker searched by candlelight the rumpled blankets covering Razz's cot. The feed sack containing his belongings was on the floor beside it. She looked inside, then checked his coat pockets and found a glove. Wood chips clung to it.

"Sueker?"

She swung around. "You scared me!"

"What're you doing up here?" Razz asked.

"Lookin'," said Sueker.

"What for?"

"Miss Tims thinks it was you who gave that tree to the church," she told him flat out.

"What gave her that idea?"

"She saw you and Billy and Martin take tools from Dad's shed. Cuttin' tools, and here's wood chips." Sueker showed him the glove.

"You haven't seen the mate, have you?" asked Razz.

"No. Why?"

"Must have lost it, clearing the road. There was a limb on Martin's road just so you know. We borrowed Dave's tools and cut it out of the way," said Razz.

Sueker wanted to believe him. But how was it that he'd nearly beat her to the church this morning? Had he known the way?

"I looked in Parker's suitcase again. I didn't find his six dollars," she held nothing back.

"Looky here. If you're thinking what I think you're thinking, just say so, and I'll go home," said Razz in a flare of temper.

"It was your idea to look again. I didn't find it. That's all I'm saying."

"I wish you'd try and remember you're a Tucker. Because Tuckers stick together," Razz said, and he turned for the stairs.

"Where're you goin'?"

"Downstairs. Maggie's looking for you. She's ready for pageant practice."

"Are you comin' too?" asked Sueker.

"No."

"You aren't going home, are you?" she said in a small voice.

"Not unless you want me to."

"I don't, Razz! I've waited and waited for you to come. I'm sorry if I hurt your feelings. It was Miss

Tims's words that upset me. I wish you'd come to practice," she pleaded.

"Not tonight. I've got stuff to do. But I'll be there Christmas Eve."

"You promise?" asked Sueker.

Razz gave her his word, and still Sueker had trouble concentrating at pageant practice. It didn't help that Parker had tagged along. He sat on the front row right next to Maggie, who was prompting kids when they forgot their lines.

Afterwards the other children clamored to decorate the tree. Mrs. O'Neida said no, that it was beautiful just the way God made it.

Sueker looked up into the green branches. She remembered going to the woods with Pa and Razz when she was little, chips flying as Pa brought down a pine tree with his ax. *Timber!* they had cheered as it shook the ground.

Then they dragged it home with their pony and had a happy Christmas. This morning she'd felt certain this Christmas was going to be the happiest yet.

That had changed. Miss Tims's words had felled her trust in her brother. Sueker was afraid to say anymore about the tree to Razz. He might go home, and she'd never see him again.

On the way home Maggie held Parker's hand. "Do you want to be in the play, Parker?"

He shook his head "no."

"Are you sure? You wouldn't have to say any lines. You could just stand up there beside Sueker."

"I can't," he said.

"Why not?" Sueker spoke up.

"You won't let them in," Parker said to Sueker. "You're mean."

"I am not mean! I'm playing a part," said Sueker.

"Yes, and you're very good at it. Why's that, I wonder?" said Maggie.

Sueker couldn't answer back without showing her hurt. She jammed her hands in her hands in her pockets and prayed Parker's brother Junior would come back and get him . . . and fast.

CHAPTER 19

The next morning Dad and Maggie left for the garage without the sales ledger—the one where the cash and the carries were tallied.

"I need you to take it to them, darlin'," said Mama as Sueker finished breakfast. "What's keeping Parker?"

"He doesn't want to go to school," said Sueker.

"I'll go see about him. Maybe he can check-see on Miss Tims. Then I'll walk him to school."

"You never walk me to school," said Sueker.

"You'd leave me in the dust gettin' there," said Mama.

It was true. Most mornings, Sueker couldn't get to school fast enough. But not today. She was tuckered out from remembering she was a Tucker.

"You don't want to be marked tardy. Why don't you ride Maggie's bike? It'll save you some time," added Mama.

"The ledger! We've been looking all over for that," said Maggie when Sueker dropped the ledger on the counter. "Hey, Dad. Look what Sueker brought us!" cried Maggie.

It hit Sueker then. Searching Razz's room had only churned up hurt, worry, fear, and confusion. The place she needed to search was so close by. She could see the trees from Dad's garage.

Sueker pointed Maggie's bicycle toward the cemetery. She pedaled with the wind in her face. Was that a space where an evergreen tree should be? The void grew larger with each turn of her tires.

Sueker leaned the bike against the cemetery gate. She continued on foot toward the windbreak. When she neared the break in the border of Christmas trees, she came upon trampled snow. Wood chips, sawdust, and a fresh cut stump hit her heart hard. But the glove she found on her way back sunk it.

On her way back to town Sueker saw the sheriff's car coming toward her. He had a passenger. It was Miss Tims.

Sueker dried her eyes on her coat sleeve and pedaled on to school.

CHAPTER 20

The morning passed. At lunch Sueker saw Parker sitting by himself and joined him. His silence suited her better than the lively chatter of her friends.

Inch by inch the day crawled by without a whisper about the tree, the cemetery, or her brother, Razz.

It was the same at home.

After supper Sueker had trouble concentrating on her homework. Afterwards she squeezed between Parker and Mama for family devotions. Razz sat across the room. His glove was in her coat pocket. Would he be angry? Would he go home the way he'd threatened? Uncertain what she should do, she did nothing.

But the next day Sueker came home from school to learn that Miss Tims had filed a complaint against Razz, Billy, Martin, and Wesley.

The punishment was five dollars or ten days in jail.

Five dollars *each*. It was a lot of money.

Maggie blamed it all on Razz. She said Wesley admitted to giving his pals and Razz a ride out to the cemetery. But how was he to know Razz had talked them into cutting down a tree?

Sueker hid her face and her hurt feelings in the bib of Mama's apron. "It's all Miss Tims's fault," she wailed.

"Because she wants justice done? No, darlin'. Miss Tims isn't to blame. Taking what doesn't belong to you is against the law, and the law must be upheld."

"I don't want to help her ever again," sobbed Sueker.

After supper Mama sent Parker over to check-see on Miss Tim.

While he was gone, Martin's mom stopped by the house. She was on her way to pay Martin's fine. She said that Billy's folks had also scratched the money together to free Billy. But Wesley's couldn't . . . or wouldn't.

"It's a crying shame. Wesley's a good boy. But it looks like he'll be spending Christmas in jail." Martin's mother said some things about Razz then. Her words were so sharp that Sueker went upstairs and knocked on Maggie's closed door.

"What do you want?" called Maggie.

Sueker couldn't say for sure except that she didn't want a closed door between them. She knocked again.

"Go away," said Maggie.

"Is Clarisse in there?" asked Sueker.

Maggie opened the door wide enough to give her Clarisse. Then she closed it again.

Sueker crossed to her own room.

Jail must be lonely too.

Razz had come all this way to see her. Now he was locked up and couldn't even come to her pageant.

CHAPTER 21

The next morning, Sueker asked if she could see Razz. Mama and Parker went along with her. Mama spoke to the sheriff. He agreed to let Sueker visit Razz for a few minutes.

"Shall we wait for you, darlin'?" asked Mama.

"No thanks, Mama. I'll be fine," she said. So Mama continued on her way, walking Parker to school.

Razz was alone in the cell.

"Where's Wesley?" Sueker asked him.

"Your brother admitted that Wesley wasn't in on the tree cuttin'. I let him go," the sheriff answered for Razz.

"Maggie was right. She said Wesley wasn't in on it," said Sueker, as the sheriff left her alone with Razz.

"Is she sore at me?" asked Razz.

"You better know it! Taking that tree *and* getting Wesley and his friends in trouble," said Sueker.

"What's that got to do with her?" asked Razz.

"You made her hang her head, that's what!"

"I was only trying to make Christmas special for you," said Razz.

"Me?" yelped Sueker.

"You're the one wanting presents, a tree, and a great big fuss, aren't you?" reminded Razz.

"A *stolen* tree is the wrong kind of fuss!" shouted Sueker.

"Is there a problem?" asked the sheriff

"Yes, and it's him!" cried Sueker as the sheriff came to see.

"I reckon this cell isn't big enough for the both of us. Would you show her out, sir?" asked Razz. He flung himself down on his cot and turned his face to the wall.

Sueker felt like he'd slapped her. She shifted her feet and swallowed the knot in her throat. What if he went away once he'd served his sentence? What if she never saw him again? Would he forget he even had a sister? She waited and waited. But he wouldn't even look at her.

The sheriff held the cell door for Sueker. She had no choice but to step out.

"Bye, Sueker T. Tilton," Razz called in a mocking voice.

For once Sueker didn't want to go to school. All day she worried that her classmates knew what Razz had done. That they were whispering behind her back.

Once school was out her worries shifted to home. What she'd told Razz in anger was true. He had brought trouble to her foster family. Maggie wasn't the only one he'd embarrassed. She'd seen Mama flush when Martin's mother raised the roof.

Sueker was almost home when Parker stopped short. She looked, and what did she see? The tree from church. It was lying in Miss Tims's front yard!

CHAPTER 22

"What's that tree doing in Miss Tims's yard?" Sueker asked as Parker trailed her into the kitchen.

Mama turned from the stove. "Pastor didn't think it was wise to keep it. So he dragged it behind the church. How it ended up in Miss Tims's front yard, I don't know."

"What's she need with it? She's got no Christmas in her," said Sueker.

"That's enough, Sueker. You're being disrespectful," reproved Mama.

With everything else that was going wrong, Sueker couldn't stand to have Mama cross with her. She ducked her head and said she was sorry.

"Is it Miss Tims's tree?" asked Parker.

"I reckon it is," replied Mama. "Would you go see if she needs anything, please, Parker?"

Sueker hadn't softened toward Miss Tims. Still it gave her a twinge to see the little hound-pup prince setting off for next door.

Sueker was at the woodpile when Parker came home from helping Miss Tims.

"There's a tree up there." He pointed toward the railroad tracks.

"So?" she pretended disinterest.

"A Christmas tree," he said.

"Are you sure?" she asked.

Parker nodded and started up the ditch.

Sueker set aside the kindling bucket and followed. It was a hedge tree on its side near the water tank. She would have walked right by it, if Parker hadn't stopped.

"You mean this?" asked Sueker. "The section men cut it down."

"Do they need it?"

"What for? It isn't good for anything but hedge," said Sueker.

"It has needles." Parker pointed to a prickly cluster.

"Those are thorns." Sueker crammed her cold hands into her coat pockets.

"We can decorate it."

Sueker gave the tree a second look. Christmas wooed her once again. Any tree was better than nothing. The tumbleweed tree had taught her that much.

Together she and Parker dragged the hedge tree home.

When supper dishes were washed and put away, Sueker told Mama and Dad that they had a surprise. They agreed to wait in the kitchen until further notice.

Parker held the front door. Sueker dragged the thorn tree into a corner of the parlor. When asked, Maggie helped them hammer together a tree stand. She snagged her dress and pricked her finger standing the tree up in the corner.

"It's a sorry looking thing," she grumbled and marched up the stairs to fix her dress.

Sueker and Parker gathered the paper decorations from around the house and hung them from thorns. Gold buttons from Mama's button tin was all the sparkle Sueker could find. Then Parker got an idea. He went upstairs and returned with the jewelry box that had belonged to his mother.

The baubles inside glistened in the lamplight. Bracelets, earrings, pins, and pearls.

"Ooh! That's pretty! Prettier even than an angel chain!" Sueker couldn't hold back her pleasure as Parker hung a strand of delicate beads on the tree.

Next he clipped a pair of ruby red earrings to a thorn cluster. Sueker's fingers itched to touch the bright jewels. But Parker placed every treasure on the thorny tree without asking for her help. The tree was transformed!

Sueker called her folks in to see. Mama clapped her hands in delight, while Dad circled the tree. He whistled in admiration.

"Would you look at that!" he exclaimed. Festive feelings flickered about Sueker like fireflies on a

warm summer night. She was sorry she'd quarreled with Razz. Seemed unfair he was here, and yet so far away. It was all that stood between them and Christmas as it ought to be.

CHAPTER 23

Sueker overheard Dad talking down in the kitchen. He told Mama he had enough money left after paying the fuel man to cover Razz's fine.

"It's awful hard on Sueker," said Mama. "But if we do, are we hindering Razz?"

Dad said something about grace.

"Let's rest on it," said Mama, which meant they would pray.

But nothing was said about it in the morning. And Razz didn't come home. Time was running out.

The next evening Sueker waited until Dad had gone to bed. Then she tiptoed down to the kitchen.

"What's *grace* mean?" she asked as Mama took the pins from her hair.

"Means getting better than what we deserve," replied Mama.

"That's what I thought." Sueker balanced on one cold foot, thinking about grace. "Why would God bring Razz all this way just to spend Christmas in jail?"

"It was Razz's wrongdoing that put him there," said Mama. She lay her hairbrush aside and pulled Sueker close. "I'm sorry, darlin'. Pray. That's all I know to tell you. God works in human hearts when we pray."

Sueker climbed the stairs to Maggie's room. Parker crept in on whispery feet. She tightened her grip on Clarisse.

"Will there be presents under our tree?" he asked.

"No. Mama says no fuss."

Sueker waited for him to leave. When he didn't, she told him about her real father and how they celebrated Christmas when he was still alive.

"Did you have a Christmas party?" Parker asked.

"No," said Sueker. "Did you?"

He nodded.

Sueker was still awake thinking about it when Maggie came home from helping Mrs. O'Neida.

"Let's have a party after the pageant," she said.

"After all the fuss over that Razz's mischief?" said Maggie. "You can't be serious. Folks are mad at Miss Tims and mad at the sheriff and the boys and mad at . . . well, they're mad. That's all."

"Maybe a party would help them stop being mad," said Sueker.

"Go to sleep, Sueker," huffed Maggie

Sueker knew then that if there was to be a party, it would have to be a surprise.

CHAPTER 24

After Saturday lunch Sueker and Parker went knocking. Sueker invited friends, neighbors, teachers, the postman, Pastor and Mrs. O'Neida. She even invited Martin's mother, who had been so snippy, calling Razz a troublemaker.

They were almost home when Parker pointed out Miss Tims's house.

"I didn't forget, I just don't want to ask her," said Sueker.

But he was right. If there was to be a true Christmas truce, she had to invite Miss Tims. Squaring her shoulders, Sueker marched up to the door.

"Susan! I was hoping you would stop by," greeted Miss Tims. "Could you and Parker move that tree off my yard, please?"

"I didn't come to do chores," said Sueker.

"You're angry with me over your brother," she stated.

Sueker didn't deny it.

Miss Tims crossed her arms. "Suppose they had taken something of yours, Susan. Your doll for instance."

"I didn't come to talk about that either," replied Sueker.

"What is it then?" asked Miss Tims stiffly.

"There's going to be a party at our house after the pageant tonight. Everybody's invited."

"I don't care much for parties. Now about that tree. When will you be able to move it?"

"Parker's too little, and I don't want to," Sueker told her.

"Very well then," said Miss Tims. And she closed her door.

Would she tell Mama and Dad on her? Sueker's face twitched. "See there? That'll teach me to listen to you," she said to Parker.

CHAPTER 25

Maggie went to church early so she and Mrs. O'Neida wouldn't be rushed. Washing dishes fell to Sueker and Parker. Afterwards they dressed in their Sunday best.

"I sure am looking forward to this pageant, Sueker. I know you're going to do a good job," said Dad.

Eager not to disappoint, Sueker walked beside him as they left the house for church. Mama and Parker followed. Just ahead was Miss Greer Tims *tap-tap-tapping* down the walk with her go-to-town cane.

"This walk's treacherous in the dark. See if she wants help, darlin'," Mama said to Sueker.

"I'll help her," Dad offered. "Run on ahead and get into your costume, Sueker."

His words put wings on Sueker's feet. She cut around Miss Tims and on to church.

Lamplight shone friendly through the windows. Pastor held the door and greeted her warmly. The tumbleweed tree drew her eyes, but couldn't hold them for long.

Up front a plank stable spilled dusty straw everywhere. There was a door beside it. On the door was a lettered sign, *INN*.

Sueker slipped into her costume and took her place behind the door. She peeked out to see Maggie with the script in her lap ready to prompt. The hat on her head belonged to Mama. The reading glasses too.

Dad came up the center aisle, helping Miss Tims. He seated her beside Maggie. Mama and Parker joined them on the front pew.

The church filled up fast. Crowded as it was, it would have held Razz. He'd come so far, and he'd promised. Sueker pushed the thought away as Mrs. O'Neida sat down at the piano.

Pastor strode to the front and welcomed the audience, and then sat down. The lights dimmed.

Miss O'Neida played "Silent Night." She stroked the keys softly.

Up the center aisle came angels singing. Toddler angels tripping along in their feed-bag gowns. Taller angels with homemade halos. Singing. All singing.

A classmate of Sueker's narrated the Christmas story.

Mary and Joseph came slowly up the aisle. Mary's face glowed with the honor of acting out the most coveted role among the girls. She put a shy hand on Joseph's arm. He helped her up the steps to the platform.

They stopped right in front of Sueker's door. The music stopped too. The candlelit stage was a holy place with all those angels and all that hush. Joseph drew forward another step and knocked.

Sueker stepped out from behind the door.

"We need a place to stay," said Joseph.

"No room." She belted her line loud and clear.

"But we've traveled so far," said Joseph.

"No room!" Sueker thundered again and sneaked a peek at Dad.

He was sitting tall, enjoying her moment.

But Parker shrank in the pew.

Distracted, she shifted her feet. What was Joseph waiting for anyway?

"Sueker," prompted Maggie from the front row.

"No room!" Sueker said, and watched Parker cover his face as she turned them away.

But that was how it happened in the Bible.

Could she help it God came to a world full of meanies? Razz, pushing her away with his words. Miss Tims. Junior Bishop, dropping off his brother like a stray pup, and Mama expecting her to make him welcome. A world of meanies . . . and she was one of them.

Stricken, she said, "There's room in the barn. It's a nice warm barn. I sleep there myself sometimes."

"Sueker! Stick to the script," Maggie said in a stage whisper.

"Say it correctly, Susan," Miss Tims chimed, clear as a bell.

Sueker looked at her there on the front row with her family. Behind them sat Pop Snow, the postman, and some other folks she had yet to invite to the party. She needed to tell Mama and Dad too. It would be okay. They'd understand. They always made room. From now on she would too. Beginning with Parker. She looked right at him and said, "There's going to be a party later and everyone's invited."

"A donkey, a cow, and some shepherds," called out Pop Snow, who liked to make folks laugh. "Sounds like a barn warming to me."

"Don't forget baby Jesus," someone else chimed in.

"I've delivered enough babies, I can tell you, it's no party," Doc Yordy spoke up.

Laughter rippled through the audience in a warm gentle wave.

"I mean at our house," said Sueker. Anxious that everyone understand they were invited, she added, "The party is at our house, and everyone's invited."

Mama looked as if she had swallowed a gnat.

But Dad said, "That's a fine idea." He came out of the pew and faced the audience. "We sure *would* like it if you could stop by a while."

"Could we finish the pageant first, Dave?" asked Pop Snow.

And they did, once the laughter faded.

CHAPTER 26

Pastor came up front at the conclusion of the pageant.

"What a magnificent program!" He lead the audience in applauding the cast, Mrs. O'Neida, Maggie, and everyone who had helped make the evening possible. Then he turned and smiled at Sueker.

"Thank you for the party invitation, Sueker. A Christmas party is a fitting reminder of all we have to look forward to when Jesus comes again. Now *that* will be a party to end all parties. And yes, Sueker, everyone is invited. Have you accepted God's invitation in the person of His Son?" he asked the audience. Then he bowed his head and closed with prayer.

Sueker changed out of her costume and pulled on her coat. She found Parker holding the door for Miss Tims.

"Are you coming to our house?" he asked.

"No thank you, Parker. I have business downtown," replied Miss Tims.

"But it's Christmas Eve," Sueker protested.

"Hurry home, Susan. A good hostess doesn't keep her guests waiting." Miss Tims turned with a tap of her cane and headed toward the business district.

Once home Parker fetched wood for the parlor stove. Sueker opened the damper on the kitchen range. She was fanning the embers to life when Maggie burst in.

"Mama's coming. I'm sure glad I'm not you," she said to Sueker.

Maggie wheeled around at the sound of Mama stamping the snow off her shoes. "Half the town's coming, Mama! Where're we going to put them? That's what I want to know!"

"Take their wraps upstairs please, Maggie. But first bring down some chairs. Wait just a minute, Sueker," Mama added as Sueker jumped to help. "I want to talk to you and Parker."

"I'm sorry! We should have asked first," Sueker said quickly.

"We'll talk about that later," said Mama. "I just want to say how much I enjoyed the pageant. You did a fine job, Sueker. I'm ashamed to think I'd said there'd be no fuss this Christmas."

The scent of lye soap, lilac water, and grace was all mixed up in Mama's glad hug.

"There's popcorn drying in the attic. Run and get it, Sueker. That's my girl. And fetch Dad's mouth harp while you're upstairs. I sure would enjoy hearing him play."

"Where is he?" asked Sueker.

"He'll be along shortly. Hurry now while I trim the lamps and light up the house."

Wesley's, Billy's, and Martin's families arrived in a cluster. Sueker came down with Dad's harmonica just as Maggie was taking their coats.

Martin's father brought his fiddle along. "Do you know the words to 'Come Christmas Morn,' Sueker?" he asked.

"Sorry, sir, I don't," she said.

"Since when did that stop yah? Just make 'em up as you go along," said Pop Snow. He cackled and slapped his knee.

"Don't you be teasing her, Pop. You did a fine job, Sueker," said Martin's mama. Then she turned around and said to mama. "Your girl did a good job in the pageant."

Mama thanked her with a hug, and replied, "Sueker's a blessing, to be sure."

Grown-ups filled the parlor and spilled into the dining room. At Mama's direction, the men pushed furnishings aside to make more room. Maggie suggested they move the tree out on the porch. But Mama wouldn't hear of it. "We'll hang it from the ceiling, if we have to," she said.

Wesley and his pals did just that. They hung it upside down halfway up the stairs. The jewels fell and the ornaments too. The children milled on the stairs, picking them up and redecorating the upside-down tree.

Guests with instruments gathered where the tree had been and led folks on a rollicking sing-along. Parker and the small boys played Pounce, a game of pegs and dried peas and pan lids. Maggie and Wesley popped popcorn. Sueker helped serve it along with cups of cold water.

Afterwards Sueker fetched Clarisse downstairs. She was playing house with her friends when Dad came in through the laundry room.

"I brought you something. Don't peek," he said and put his hands over her eyes.

"What kind of something?" she cried.

Dad took his hands away.

And there stood Razz.

CHAPTER 27

Sueker squealed and flung herself at Razz.

"Merry Christmas from Miss Tims!" called Dad.

"Miss Tims?" gasped Sueker, clinging to Razz. "*She* paid your way out?"

Razz untangled himself from her hug. "Dave tried, didn't you Dave?"

"Yes, I did. But Miss Tims had another idea," said Dad. "Tell her, Razz."

"First, she gave me a tongue-lashing. Said I was thoughtless and brash and . . . I don't know what all," said Razz.

"If she felt that way, why'd she pay your fine?"

"She didn't. She talked the sheriff into letting her be my substitute for a while."

"You don't mean . . ."

"Yes, Miss Tims is taking my place in jail. She did it for you," added Razz. "She called you a lily."

"She's talking about my name. It means 'lily'," said Sueker.

"Yes, and she says that we ought not to waste such a name as that. And one more thing." Razz reached into his coat pocket. "I'm supposed to give you this."

It was a slim package wrapped in plain brown paper. Sueker peeled the paper back. It was Miss Tims's book of names.

Why would she give away what she valued so highly? Mystified, Sueker opened the cover with careful hands.

"Is my name in there?" Razz asked, before Sueker could look up her own.

It wasn't.

"Sorry," she said. "You're not in the book."

Kids and grown-ups called out their names. Sueker couldn't turn pages fast enough. Too bad Miss Tims couldn't be there to see the pleasure her gift brought everyone.

Sueker was sorry to see the party end. But happy too. God had satisfied every longing. Dad and Razz pushed the furniture back in place. The thorn tree too. Once again the trimmings fell.

This time they decorated it as a family. Sueker and Mama and Maggie and Parker and Dad and Razz. They chattered about the party, sharing stories and smiles, and enjoying the afterglow until time for Razz to keep his word.

Dad went along to see Miss Tims safely home.

Sueker wished Razz didn't have to go. Good thing it was time for bed. She could no more hide her tears than pretty baubles could disguise a tree's thorns.

Parker was on the landing with Clarisse under his arm and Mama holding his hand.

"Give her here," said Sueker, reaching for her doll.

"It's hers, darlin'," said Mama gently.

Sueker was ready for Parker to plead, but he gave her the doll and went on to bed.

Sueker crawled in with Maggie, itching on the inside. The remorse she'd felt earlier was in a tug of war with her right of ownership.

"Maggie? Are you asleep?" she whispered.

"I'm trying."

"Me, too. But I can't," said Sueker.

Maggie asked why. It was hard to tell Maggie how she felt about Parker. But when she did, Maggie surprised her.

"I used to feel the same way about you. But Mama said God would help me if I'd make room."

"Room for *me*, you mean?" asked Sueker.

"For God," said Maggie.

Sueker knew what Maggie's answer had been. She could see His love in Mama and Dad too. It wasn't that they had more room. It was what they did with the room they had. They let God fill it.

Sueker said her thank-yous to God. She left Clarisse with Parker and went downstairs to share what she'd prayed.

"I asked God to help me make room," she whispered in Mama's ear.

"That's my girl. He'll help you for sure." Mama patted her lap.

Sueker had outgrown it, but she perched there anyway. They were talking about Miss Tims's present when Dad came home. Learning of Sueker's contrite heart, he spoke of a book God kept.

"In it He records the names of the redeemed," Dad told her.

"Do you know what it means to be redeemed?" asked Mama.

When Dad told her, Sueker could see that asking God to take away her jealousy didn't go far enough. She wanted her name in the Book of Life. It was the only gift she couldn't live without.

CHAPTER 28

The next day was Sunday. Sueker went forward and made public her new life in Jesus. She was sorry Razz couldn't be there. Dad went with her to see him that afternoon.

Sueker took along Miss Tims's book of names. She showed Razz where she'd written in his name. Beside it in parentheses she had scrawled, *Sueker's brother.* Razz grinned. "Tell me something I don't know."

So Sueker told him about God's book of names. Dad helped her explain.

Then he asked Razz if he knew how to receive Jesus as his Savior.

Razz said he'd been thinking about it, but that he had some things to work through first. Then he reminded Dad that his foster father was the preacher in Shirley.

"He's a fine fellow. I hope you'll give him my greetings. And Razz?" added Dad. "Jail isn't the only freedom stealer. Jesus will keep your heart right, if you'll let Him."

Razz served his time and returned to Sueker's family. It took him two days to clear the tree from Miss Tims's lawn. Once he'd chopped it into firewood, Sueker and Parker stacked it on her wood pile.

Two days later Razz helped a trucker friend of Dad's load his trailer. In return the trucker agreed to give Razz a ride east.

Sueker was there to see him off. She was saying good-bye when Razz put six silver dollars in her hand.

"Would you give that to Parker for me?"

"You *did* take it then?" Sueker's heart plunged. "Razz! Why'd you do that?"

Razz jutted out his chin. "I figured if I didn't look after myself, who would? But I've been thinking. Jail's no place for a Tucker."

Razz dutch-rubbed her head and climbed into the waiting truck.

The driver let off the brake. The truck rolled forward.

"Keep those letters comin', you hear?" Razz called out the window. "And quit that sniffling. You're mostly Tucker, remember?"

Parker was waiting for Sueker at the corner. His teeth were chattering.

"If you close your coat, there's a chance you won't blow away," she told him and dried her face with her sleeve.

He fumbled with the buttons until Sueker thought they'd both freeze. She did it for him. Then she gave him his dollars and told him she was wrong and that he'd been right about Razz.

Parker put his money in his pocket and his tongue in the hole where his tooth had been. "I know your real name."

"Miss Tims tell you? She doesn't believe in nicknames," Sueker said when he nodded.

"Pup's a little dog," said Parker.

"Miss Tims again, I'm guessing," said Sueker.

"Yes," said Parker. He looked at her then and asked, "Can it be a nickname too?"

"If you want," said Sueker. "Are you cold?"

Parker nodded.

"Me too," said Sueker. "Let's go home, Pup." And she took his hand.